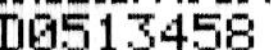
D0513458

C334127620

LAST TREE in the CITY

For Thomas, Joanne and Michael

PC

First published in the UK in 2017
by New Frontier Publishing (Europe) Pty. Ltd.
93 Harbord Street, London SW6 6PN
www.newfrontierpublishing.co.uk

ISBN: 978-1-912076-55-0

A CIP catalogue record for this book is available from the British Library.

Printed in China
10 9 8 7 6 5 4 3 2 1

PETER CARNAVAS

Edward lived in the city.

It was a place of concrete and cars,
a world without colour.

But Edward knew a part of the city that wasn't like the city at all.

At the end of his street, surrounded by old buildings,
stood the last tree in the city.

Edward would forget the concrete and the cars.

He would forget the city altogether.

For a small moment every day, Edward knew nothing but the tree.

Then the day arrived ...

when the tree was gone.

Without the tree, Edward's days were empty.
He had nowhere to go

but one day, he started pedalling anyway.

At the end of his street, surrounded by old buildings,
something warmed his heart.

A piece of the tree lay before him. There was colour in its leaves.

Edward tried to think of a place in the city to plant his tree.
By the next morning, he knew just what to do.

Edward knew a part of the city that wasn't like the city at all and he carried it everywhere.

Then something wonderful happened ...